Children's Nativity

The Christmas Story through a Child's Eyes

RICHARD SURMAN

HarperCollins*Publishers*

The cast in order of appearance:

Narrator   *Olivia*
Joseph   *Kit*
Mary   *Rachael*
Angel one   *Annabel*
Angel two   *Lucy*
Innkeeper   *Poppy*
Angel three   *Sara*
Angel four   *Omari*
Shepherd one   *Oliver*
Shepherd two   *Jack*
Shepherd three   *Ali*
First King   *Gabriel*
Second King   *Gregor*
Third King   *Carlos*

Helped by their teacher, Miss Noël

Introduction

I wonder how many parents have sat with lumps in their throats as they watched their children acting out the story of the Nativity. I know I have; after all, it is a story about a child, and who could be closer to that child than other children?

The children depicted in this book have used their own ideas, thoughts and perceptions in an open and unrestricted way. The result is a mix of humour, drama and the odd practical joke that complements the profound nature of the event that they are enacting. I wanted to allow my cast to bring something of themselves into the book. The result is that almost everything in this book has been either made by or suggested by the children who took part. The costumes are home made, as are the scenery and props. The dialogue was observed by being a 'fly on the wall' when the cast was preparing for rehearsals. So in every way this play belongs to the children, and I am obliged to them for such exuberant input.

My thanks to all the children who took part. In particular I want to thank my sons, Carlos and Gabi, for their ideas about scenery and props, and for Carlos's excellent menagerie designs. I am also very grateful to Catherine Davenport for helping me when I ran out of children, and to my wife Blanca for running the refreshments and controlling the wild background activity that sometimes accompanied rehearsals.

So, if you are sitting comfortably, the cast is as ready as they will ever be, and now I shall hand you over to our narrator, Olivia.

Welcome to our Nativity Play! We've been very busy preparing this play this year, and the cast are just putting the finishing touches to their costumes. One of the three wise men has the 'flu, and Gabriel has kindly taken his place at the last minute. All the costumes have been designed by us, with the help of our teacher, Miss Noël, and all the scenery and props have been designed and

made by Carlos. We hope that you will enjoy the hard work that has been put into this year's production. After the play has finished we will invite you to join us in singing some Christmas carols.

Tonight we are going to tell the story of a very special baby who was born just over 2000 years ago. It is the story of the first Christmas, when God sent his Son to us. In a country called Galilee, in the small town of Nazareth, there lived a carpenter named Joseph. He made all sorts of things for people, like tables and chairs. Joseph was going to marry Mary.

I'm going to the workshop.

Make sure you're home for lunch.

One day, when Joseph was at his workshop, Mary was at home when an angel came through the window. Mary was quite surprised, but the angel told her not to worry. The angel also said that God had chosen her to have a very special baby.

When Joseph came back for his lunch, Mary told him what had happened. They were both very happy, and started to prepare for when the baby was born.

Don't worry, Mary, I'm the angel Gabriel and this is my friend.

Where did you come from?

Some time later, they heard that the Roman Emperor Augustus Caesar wanted to find out how many people lived in his empire, and that everyone would have to go to certain towns to be counted.

Joseph and Mary were not pleased, as they would have to travel to Bethlehem. They set off and it was a cold and long journey through the mountains. Mary found it especially hard as her baby was going to be born very soon.

Cheer up, Mary, we're nearly there.

I wish we hadn't sold that donkey. I'm tired and cold.

Many people passed them on their journey, and Joseph knew that it was not going to be easy to find shelter. Eventually they arrived in Bethlehem and, sure enough, all the hotels and inns were full.

Joseph, we've already tried this one.

I'm going to have one more try.
There must be somewhere we can stay.

After walking round and round the town, they tried one last time, and knocked on the door of an inn. The innkeeper wasn't very happy to be woken up but, when he saw how close Mary was to having her baby, he told them that they could stay in a small stable round the back of his inn.

All right, all right, I'm coming.
Why can't I get one night's peaceful sleep?

Look, we're desperate. My wife is going to have a baby. Don't you even have an old shed?

Oh, it's you again. I've already told you I'm full ... but wait a moment. There's a stable down the lane. You can sleep there, but don't upset the animals.

Joseph tried to make the stable as comfortable as possible for Mary. He made a soft bed of straw for her, which he covered with a blanket. He also found a basket that he filled with straw so that the baby would have a warm bed. The animals in the stable didn't seem to mind having them there.

During the night the baby was born. It was a boy. Mary and Joseph were very happy, because they knew that God had sent his Son to the world. When the baby cried, the animals in the stable woke up. They were very curious and kept staring at the baby. Mary told Joseph that God wanted them to call the baby Jesus, and the three of them settled down to keep warm through the cold night.

Not far away, on a cold hillside overlooking Bethlehem, there were some shepherds. In those days shepherds would stay out at night with their sheep to protect them from bandits and wolves. All of a sudden an angel appeared.

Um ... Miss Noël? Can you get Harmony off the stage?

I think there's someone behind me.

Huh! Sisters!

The shepherds were scared out of
their wits, but the angel told them
not to be afraid. She said she had
come to tell them that the Son of
God had been born, and that they
should go to Bethlehem to see him.

Look! Olivia!

Look! Angels!

The shepherds decided that they must go to see this marvellous baby, and they set off down the hill towards Bethlehem. When they reached the town, the shepherds looked everywhere, and were just about to give up when one of them saw a stable.

There's the baby the angel told us about.

As they got closer they saw Mary, Joseph and the baby Jesus.
The shepherds were filled with joy and wonder. One of them
gave a baby lamb for Jesus to have as a pet. Jesus smiled at them.

Hark the herald angels sing!

Meanwhile, others were looking for the baby Jesus too. Far to the west, in a strange and distant land, three wise men had been wondering about a bright new star that had appeared in the sky.

The string's snapped

Where's the star?

We can't just stand here!

Look, yonder star is coming.

About time too.

Let's get going.

They had spent many weeks wondering what it meant, and then decided to follow the star. After long journeys through deserts and over mountains, the three wise men came near to Bethlehem. They saw that the star had stopped moving and was shining down brightly on a small stable.

They were very excited, and rushed to the stable. When they saw the baby Jesus they became very quiet, and knelt before him. They knew in their hearts that God had sent this special child to show his love for everyone.

At last, here is the child we seek.

Hello, Gabi!

Away in a manger...

Each had a gift, which they offered to Jesus in turn: gold, frankincense and myrrh. Jesus smiled at the three wise men too. They were so excited that they left soon after, to tell everyone they could about the marvellous events in Bethlehem.

Although this happened over two thousand years ago, every Christmas since we remember how God sent us his Son, to show how much he loves us all.

Can I mend my wing?

Curtain Call

HarperCollins*Publishers*
77–85 Fulham Palace Road, London W6 8JB
www.fireandwater.com

First published in Great Britain in 2000 by HarperCollins*Publishers*

1 3 5 7 9 8 6 4 2

Copyright © 2000 Richard Surman

Richard Surman asserts the moral right to be identified
as the author and photographer of this work.

A catalogue record for this book is
available from the British Library.

ISBN 0 00 628124 9

Printed and bound in Belgium by Proost NV, Turnhout